Bradley jumped off his bed and knelt next to Brian. The dead tree was hidden from sight. The neighbors had draped a huge blue tarp around the tree. The tarp hung from the branches all the way to the ground. It was like a big blue tent with the tree inside.

Suddenly a light went on inside the tarp, making it glow. Mr. and Mrs. Sargent were in there. Bradley could see their shapes moving around.

"I don't think they're building a swimming pool," Brian whispered.

"And they're not making a garden, either," Bradley said. "So what *are* they doing?"

"What if Mr. and Mrs. Sargent are spies?" Brian whispered. "Or bank robbers! Maybe they're burying money they stole in their latest robbery! We need to get inside that tarp!"

Calendar Mysteries

November Night

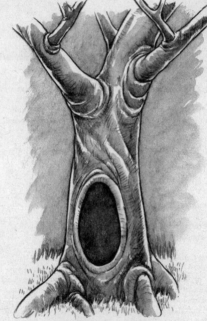

by **Ron Roy**

illustrated by
John Steven Gurney

A STEPPING STONE BOOK™

Random House 🏠 New York

*I dedicate this book to kind children
who do nice things for other people.*
—R.R.

To Hana and Adelaide
—J.S.G.

Text copyright © 2014 by Ron Roy
Cover art, map, and interior illustrations copyright © 2014 by John Steven Gurney

Visit us on the Web!
ronroy.com
randomhouse.com/kids

Educators and librarians, for a variety of teaching tools, visit us at
RHTeachersLibrarians.com

Library of Congress Cataloging-in-Publication Data
Roy, Ron.
November night / by Ron Roy ; illustrated by John Steven Gurney. — First edition.
pages cm. — (Calendar mysteries ; 11)
"A Stepping Stone book"
Summary: "As Thanksgiving approaches, Nate and Lucy must help Bradley and
Brian find out what their shady new neighbors are up to." —Provided by publisher.
ISBN 978-0-385-37165-0 (trade) — ISBN 978-0-385-37166-7 (lib. bdg.) —
ISBN 978-0-385-37167-4 (ebook)
[1. Mystery and detective stories. 2. Neighbors—Fiction. 3. Thanksgiving Day—
Fiction. 4. Twins—Fiction. 5. Brothers and sisters—Fiction. 6. Cousins—Fiction.]
I. Gurney, John Steven, illustrations. II. Title.
PZ7.R8139Nov 2014
[Fic]—dc23 2013020099

Printed in the United States of America
10 9 8 7 6 5 4

This book has been officially leveled by using the F&P Text Level Gradient™ Leveling
System.

Random House Children's Books supports the First Amendment and
celebrates the right to read.

Contents

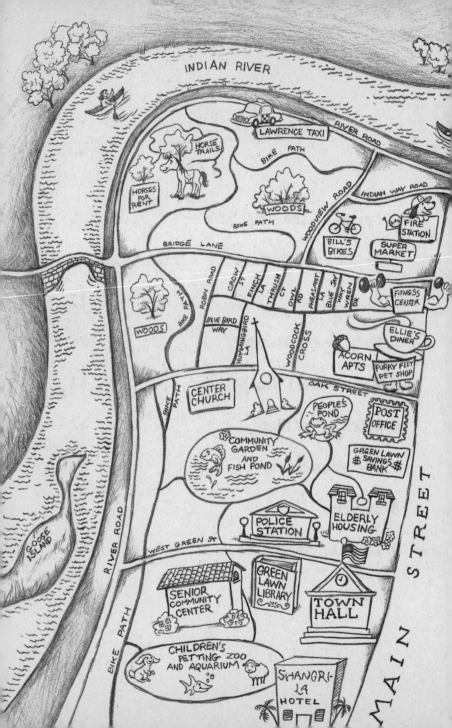

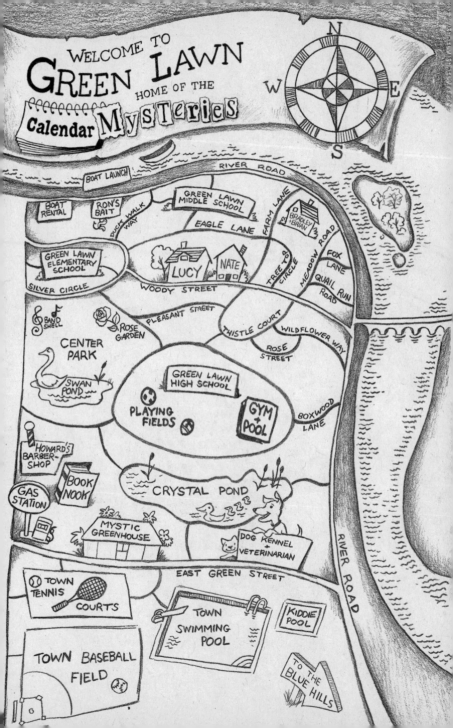

1
Spying on the Neighbors

On the Sunday before Thanksgiving,
Bradley Pinto walked into his bedroom.
His twin brother, Brian, was kneeling
in front of the window. He was peering
through binoculars.

"What are you doing?" Bradley asked.

"Nothing," Brian said.

"Yes, you are," Bradley said. "You're
spying on the new neighbors again."

"I'm not exactly spying," Brian said.
"I'm just checking them out."

Bradley flopped down on his bed.
"Mom and Dad gave us the binoculars

so we could learn about birds and nature stuff," he said.

"Looking at people is more fun," Brian said. "And I *am* learning about nature. I saw a hawk in the tree."

Bradley knelt next to his brother. He looked at the brand-new fence that surrounded the neighbors' yard. A tall dead tree stood in the middle of the backyard.

Before the new neighbors moved in, the twins used to play inside the tree's hollow trunk. The tree trunk was so big that Bradley and Brian couldn't stretch their arms around it. Sometimes, they would hide in the trunk from their older brother, Josh. Other times, the twins and their friends Nate and Lucy would sit inside and pretend they were lost in the woods. Or they'd pretend to be cave people hiding from ferocious animals.

Bradley had lined the hollow trunk with hay from Polly the pony's stall to make it softer to sit on.

Brian had invented a game called troll in the hole. He would hide inside the tree trunk, wearing a scary Halloween mask. Bradley, Nate, and Lucy would walk past, and Brian would jump out, yelling, "Troll is hungry! Troll is going to eat you!"

Nate would yell, "Don't eat me, Mr. Troll! I taste like rotten eggs!"

Bradley would yell, "Don't eat me, Mr. Troll! I taste like dirty socks!"

Lucy would just run away, laughing.

But last week, a moving van had shown up. Workers unloaded furniture and boxes. New neighbors moved in! Bradley's mom told the twins the neighbors were Mr. and Mrs. Sargent.

A few days later, a truck carrying lumber drove into the driveway. Two men spent a whole day building a tall wood fence around the neighbors' yard with slats so close together that the kids couldn't see through it. There was a wide gate so the Sargents could drive their car inside the fence.

Now the kids couldn't get into the yard. They couldn't play troll in the hole. They could just look at their favorite tree through binoculars.

"Look, there they are!" Brian cried suddenly.

On the other side of the fence were a man and woman. They had gray hair and wore sweaters and jeans. The man had on a red baseball cap. A gray ponytail stuck out the back. They stood and stared up at the old dead tree.

"Maybe they're going to cut the tree down," Bradley said.

"They better not!" Brian wailed. "What about my money?"

"What money?" Bradley asked.

Brian picked up his piggy bank and shook it. The bank was empty. "Every week, I hide my allowance money in a jar. I put the jar inside the old tree under the hay."

Bradley's eyes got wide. "Why do you hide your money?" he asked.

"So Josh won't get it!" Brian said. "He used to sneak in here and borrow money from my bank. Only he forgot to pay it back!"

They both looked out the window. "What if the new neighbors find the jar?" Brian asked. "There's twenty dollars and thirty-seven cents in it!"

"Well, what about my flashlight?" Bradley asked.

"What about it?" Brian said.

"The last time we were playing inside the tree, I left my special flashlight under the hay," Bradley said. "The one with little bats on the handle that glow in the dark!"

Just then, something huge, black, and hairy bolted out of the neighbors' back door. It charged across the yard toward the man and woman.

"Oh my gosh, a bear is attacking Mr. and Mrs. Sargent!" Brian said.

The giant hairy thing stood on its hind legs and began licking Mrs. Sargent's face.

Bradley gulped. "It's just a really big dog," he said. "I guess that's why they built the fence."

The boys' basset hound, Pal, wandered into the room. He padded over to the window and put his front paws on the sill. When he saw the neighbors' dog, he let out a low growl.

Brian patted Pal on his head. "Don't worry, boy," he said. "We'll protect you!"

Pal ran and hid under Bradley's bed.

The boys watched the neighbors walk into their garage. They came out lugging a long ladder. They leaned the ladder against the tree.

Mr. Sargent climbed up into the tree.

He unclipped a tape measure from his belt and measured the lowest branches. Mrs. Sargent wrote something on a clipboard pad. Then she unrolled a big sheet of paper. She spread it out on the ground and put rocks on the corners. Her husband came down, and they got on their

knees and studied the unrolled paper. Mrs. Sargent wrote more things on her pad.

Brian trained the binoculars onto the paper. "It's all funny drawings," he said. "Grandpa had pictures like that when he built his boat, remember?"

"Do you think they're going to build a boat?" Bradley asked.

"I don't care what they build as long as they don't cut our tree down!"

"Um, it's not our tree," Bradley said. "It's their tree now."

The boys watched the neighbors walk all around the tree. Mr. Sargent took more measurements. Mrs. Sargent wrote more things on her pad.

Mr. Sargent put his head inside the hollow part of the tree. He crawled inside, then came out again. He said something to his wife, and they both laughed. They went back to the pictures on the roll of paper. They scratched their heads.

"Don't look under the hay!" Bradley whispered.

Mr. Sargent went into the house and came out with two mugs. Bradley could see the steam rising. The neighbors sipped from their mugs and stared at their tree. They sat on the ground and leaned against the trunk.

The twins heard their mother's voice from downstairs. "Supper, you two!" she called. "And wash your hands, please."

2
Bradley's Nightmare

"You guys were pretty quiet in your room," their father said. "Were you hatching some evil plan?" He grinned.

"No, but we think the new neighbors are going to build something in their backyard," Bradley said. "They might cut the tree down!"

"How do you know?" their mother asked. She passed a plate full of fried chicken.

"Brian is spying on them with the binoculars," Bradley said.

"Mr. and Mrs. Sargent are from Florida," the boys' father said, passing the green beans to Josh. "A lot of people in Florida have swimming pools in their yards. Maybe the Sargents are going to put in a swimming pool."

"Sweet!" Josh said. "They could hire me to keep it clean."

"I'll bet they're going to plant a vegetable garden," Mrs. Pinto said. "I think Martha Sargent misses her garden in Florida."

"Mom, it's almost Thanksgiving," Bradley said. "Why would she plant a garden now?"

"You're right, honey," his mom said. "I meant in the springtime."

"Good, maybe she'll give us some of her vegetables," Mr. Pinto said.

"No way!" Josh said. "We don't need more vegetables in this house. Mom makes us eat too many already. One of these days, I'm going to turn green!"

"Like Kermit the Frog," Bradley said, grinning at Josh.

"I should invite them over for a meal," their mother said. "I think Martha and Ralph miss their kids and grandkids."

"Just don't invite their dog," Josh said. "He'd eat *us*!"

After supper, Bradley and Brian went upstairs. Brian stepped into the bathroom, and Bradley went into their bedroom and picked up his book.

"I can't wait for Thanksgiving," he said. "Only a few more days!"

"Me too," Brian said. He came out of the bathroom, wiping toothpaste off his chin. "Pumpkin pie! Ice cream! Mashed potatoes!"

He knelt in front of the window and looked outside. "Oh my gosh! Bradley, come and see!"

Bradley jumped off his bed and knelt next to Brian. The dead tree was hidden from sight. The neighbors had draped a huge blue tarp around the tree. The tarp hung from the branches all the way to the ground. It was like a big blue tent with the tree inside.

Suddenly a light went on inside the tarp, making it glow. Mr. and Mrs. Sargent were in there. Bradley could see their shapes moving around.

"I don't think they're building a swimming pool," Brian whispered.

"And they're not making a garden, either," Bradley said. "So what *are* they doing?"

"What if Mr. and Mrs. Sargent are spies?" Brian whispered. "Or bank robbers! Maybe they're burying money they stole in their latest robbery! We need to get inside that tarp!"

"We?" Bradley said.

"Yeah, you, me, Lucy, and Nate," Brian said. "Let's call them!"

Lucy Armstrong was the cousin of Josh's friend Dink. She was staying with Dink's family for a year while her parents worked on a Native American reservation in Arizona.

Nate's older sister, Ruth Rose, was Josh's other best friend. His family lived next door to Dink, so all the kids were friends.

Bradley looked at the clock. "It's too late to call," he said. "But we'll see them tomorrow morning at school." He changed into his pajamas.

"There is something weird about our new neighbors," Brian said. "And we're going to find out what!"

Bradley fell asleep thinking about what could be going on inside the strange blue tarp. He dreamed that he was climbing over the fence to get a closer look. Suddenly the giant black dog appeared out of the night. It leaped on Bradley and started to—

Bradley woke up screaming.

"It's only a nightmare," he whispered to himself. But it had seemed so real! Bradley closed his eyes and thought about Thanksgiving pumpkin pie and ice cream. Finally, he went back to sleep.

3
On the Case

At eight-thirty the next morning, Bradley and Brian met their two friends on the corner of Farm Lane and Woody Street. They always walked to school with Nate and Lucy.

"Our new neighbors are doing something strange next door!" Brian blurted out.

"Like what?" Nate asked.

"You know our favorite tree?" Brian asked. "They measured it, then covered it with this blue tarp thing. And they're doing something inside the tarp, where we can't see them! All we could see was their shadows."

"Maybe they're digging for treasure," Lucy said.

"They have a giant dog," Bradley said. "About ten times as big as Pal!" He told them about his nightmare.

"Yeah, and Bradley screamed so loud I woke up!" Brian added.

The kids hurried toward the elementary school.

"I wish I was invisible," Brian said. "Then I could climb over the fence and that big old dog wouldn't even see me!"

"But he'd still smell you," Nate said. "Then he'd follow his nose and gobble you up!"

Bradley grinned. "Maybe if you put on some of Mom's perfume, the dog would think you were a rosebush!"

"Very funny," Brian said.

They reached their school as the bell

was ringing. "We need to investigate," Brian said. "Can you come to our house right after school?"

"Sure," Lucy said. "I love solving mysteries!"

"Me too," Nate said. "But I'm not wearing any perfume!"

At three o'clock, the four kids ran back to Bradley and Brian's house on Farm Lane.

Above the backyard fence, they could see the blue tarp hanging from the tree's branches.

"I wonder if they're home," Bradley whispered.

Lucy found a knothole in the fence. "Nobody's there," she whispered. "But I can see their green car in the driveway."

"Can you see the dog?" Brian asked.

Lucy shook her head. "Nope, just a squirrel."

They each took a turn peeking

through the hole. "Guys, the Sargents are coming out of their house!" Nate said. "They're walking toward the car."

Nate looked at Bradley. "They don't look weird to me."

Brian put his eye to the hole. "Shhh, they're talking!" he whispered. "Mrs. Sargent said they're going shopping in town."

The other three kids placed their

ears against the fence. They all heard car doors slamming.

Brian was still looking through the knothole. "And Mrs. Sargent has her clipboard. She was making a list yesterday."

"Yeah," Bradley said. "I bet if we follow them, we can find out what they buy. Then we can figure out what they're doing!"

"Wait!" Brian said. "After they leave,

I can sneak over and get my jar of money!" He had told Nate and Lucy about hiding his allowance in the old tree.

"And my flashlight," Bradley added.

"What about the dog?" Nate asked.

Brian peeked through the knothole again. "Rats," he said. "The dog is sleeping under the tree!"

"Let's go to Main Street," Bradley said. "If we get there before they do, we can spy on them!"

The kids took off running. They raced down Eagle Lane, then cut through the playground at the elementary school. A few minutes later, they were on Main Street, across from the fire station.

"Stop! I have a pain in my side from running!" Nate said. He bent over and held his side.

"There they are!" Bradley said. The neighbors' green car was at the stop sign on Silver Circle. Then it turned onto Main Street. Bradley could see Mr.

Sargent driving. Mrs. Sargent sat next to him. The car pulled into the supermarket parking lot.

The kids crossed Main Street and ran to the back of the fire station. Its parking lot was next to the supermarket lot. The kids arrived just in time to see the green car turn into a space and stop.

"Are they going grocery shopping?" Nate asked.

Bradley, Brian, Nate, and Lucy were hiding behind a row of bushes. They watched Mr. and Mrs. Sargent leave their car and head to the rear of the supermarket. She was carrying the clipboard.

"They might be going to that little hardware store inside the supermarket," Brian said.

"Should we follow them?" Bradley asked.

"They'll spot us if we do," Brian said. "They must have seen us next door."

"I can go in," Lucy said. "They don't know me! Come with me, Nate."

"Good idea," Bradley said. "Find out what they buy!"

He and Brian watched Lucy and Nate scoot between some cars. They slipped into the supermarket's back door two minutes behind Mr. and Mrs. Sargent.

"I'll be right back," Bradley told Brian. He ran to the neighbors' car and peeked into the back. He saw an old blanket, a bunch of tools, and a map of Florida.

"Bradley! Come on!" Brian called. Bradley ran back to his brother. Mr. and Mrs. Sargent came out carrying bags. They headed right for their car.

The bags were lumpy. They looked heavy.

Just then, Nate and Lucy ran up to the twins.

"We got it!" Lucy said.

"Got what?" Brian asked.

"This!" Lucy said. She held out a receipt. "I saw Mr. Sargent drop this into the trash, so I grabbed it!"

The four kids huddled together and read what was on the receipt:

ROPE—20 FEET $6.50

WIRE—10 FEET $9.75

ALUMINUM—ONE ROLL $24.15

AX $12.00

PAINT $22.75

ROPE LADDER $35.00

GLASS $10.00

4
Weirder and Weirder

"An ax!" Brian said. "What's that for?"

"And it's real sharp!" Nate said. "I watched the salesman show Mr. Sargent. He shaved some hair off his own arm!"

Bradley studied the receipt. "And what's with the rope ladder?" he asked. "I don't get it."

"They're coming back!" Lucy said.

Mr. and Mrs. Sargent walked past the kids' hiding spot. Now they weren't carrying anything except the clipboard.

"They must have put the stuff in their car," Bradley said.

"Where are they going now?" Nate asked.

"Let's follow them," Brian said.

The four kids fell in behind Mr. and Mrs. Sargent. The couple walked into the gas station, and the kids hid behind some bushes. They had a perfect view of their neighbors as they chatted with Mr. Holly, the owner.

They watched Mr. Holly pull something off a shelf and hand it to Mr. Sargent.

"What is it?" Brian whispered.

"I don't know," Lucy said.

"I'll find out!" Nate said. He dashed up to a window. Nate was only six feet away from the Sargents and Mr. Holly.

A minute later, he came racing back. "It's some kind of motor," he said. "He's telling them how it runs."

"An ax and a rope ladder and a motor?" Bradley said. "Very weird!"

"Watch out. Here they come!" Lucy said.

The four spies ducked as the Sargents strolled past them. Mr. Sargent carried a box.

The kids followed, tiptoeing and silent.

Bradley tried to figure out what the Sargents could be building that needed a motor. A submarine? A car? An airplane?

The Sargents left the motor in their car, then walked up Bridge Lane to Bill's Bikes. The kids heard a little bell jingle as the neighbors stepped inside Bill's door.

"Maybe they're buying a bike," Nate said.

"They have a plan," Bradley said. "We just don't know what it is. But do you think they bought the ax to cut down that tree?"

"I don't think they can cut down that huge tree with an ax," Lucy said. "It would take them a year!"

"I hope you're right," Bradley said. Then the door of Bill's Bikes opened with another jingle. Mr. and Mrs. Sargent came out, carrying two large bags. Once again, they headed for their car.

"I wonder what's in those bags," Brian whispered.

"I'll find out!" Bradley said. He ran up to Bill's and entered the shop. The jingling bell sounded again.

Bill smiled at Bradley. "Hey, what's up?" he asked.

Bradley went over to the counter. Bill was squirting oil onto a bike chain. "You know that couple who were just in here?" he asked.

"Yep, Mr. and Mrs. Sargent. Real nice people," Bill said. "They told me they just moved up here from Florida."

"They bought the house next to ours," Bradley informed Bill. "And they're building something in the backyard. My friends and my brother and I are trying to figure out what it is."

Bill raised his eyebrows. "Why do you want to know?" he asked.

"We're playing detectives," Bradley

said. "It's kind of a mystery and we're looking for clues."

Bill grinned. "They bought a bunch of bike parts: couple of seats, some chains, and half a dozen pedals," he said.

"Do you think they're building bikes?" Bradley asked.

Bill laughed. "That's what I asked them," he said. "They told me they were working on a secret project."

Bradley thanked Bill and hurried out the door. He ran back to the other kids. "They bought bike parts," he said. *"For a secret project!"*

"Weirder and weirder," Brian said.

"There they go," Nate said. They all watched the green car pull out of the parking lot.

5
Brian's Great Escape

The kids ran back to the twins' house. Bradley peeked through the knothole in the fence. He didn't see the neighbors or their car. But the big black dog was lying under the tree with his eyes closed.

"They're not home yet," Bradley said.

"Running makes me hungry. Let's go in and get a snack," Brian said.

They trooped into the house, where they found a bowl of apples on the kitchen table. They each took one and went back outside. Brian walked over to the knothole. "Monster Dog is still sleeping," he told the other kids.

"I wonder what his name is," Bradley said.

"Probably something like *Killer*," Nate said.

Brian knocked on the fence. "Here, Killer," he called. "Good Killer, come and say hello."

Suddenly the giant dog leaped up and charged the fence. He stood on his hind legs, put his paws on the wood, and barked. His long pink tongue came through the knothole.

Bradley leaped backward. "It's just like in my nightmare!" he said.

Brian jumped, too, dropping his apple. It rolled in the dirt. "Rats," he said.

He held the dirty apple up to the knothole. "Do you like apples, Killer?" he asked the dog.

The tongue came through the knot-hole again. Brian let the dog lick the apple, and then he tossed it over the fence. They all heard the dog begin to chew.

"I guess Killer likes fruit," Lucy said.

"This gives me an idea!" Brian said. "We can get him away from the tree with our apples! Then, when he's busy eating, I can go over the fence and get my money and Bradley's flashlight."

Brian pointed at some bushes at the far end of the fence. "If we can get him to the other side of those bushes, he won't be able to see me climb over," he said.

"But he might smell you!" Lucy said.

"You'll be his Brian burger!" Nate put in.

"Don't do it," Bradley said.

"But don't you guys want to know what they're doing behind that tarp?" Brian asked. He lowered his voice. "They could be burying a dead body! We could turn them in to Officer Fallon. We'd be heroes!"

"How will you get over the fence?" Nate asked. He reached up, and his hand didn't quite touch the top of the fence. "It's about five feet tall."

"Why wouldn't you just go through the gate where they bring their car in?" Lucy asked.

"Can't," Brian said. "It's latched on the inside. But I can use Dad's new ladder. Help me get it, Bradley!" He and Bradley ran toward the barn.

Josh, Bradley, and Brian had bought their dad a shiny new aluminum ladder for his birthday. The twins came back carrying the six-foot ladder. They leaned it against the fence. "I can jump down on the other side," Brian said.

"But then how will you come back?" Lucy asked. "The ladder will be on our side of the fence."

"I didn't think about that," Brian said.

"I know!" Nate said. "Lucy will go to the corner of the fence with our apples. The dog will smell them and follow her. Bradley and I will stay here with Brian. After he goes over, Bradley and I will lift the ladder over the fence. And that's how Brian will get back into this yard."

"Excellent plan!" Brian said. "Okay, Lucy, do your stuff!"

"One teensy problem," Bradley said. "How will we get Dad's ladder back on this side again?"

"We'll figure that out later," Brian said.

Bradley and Nate handed Lucy their partly eaten apples. Lucy ran toward Meadow Road, where the fence turned a corner. She made sure she was past the bushes. Then she banged on the fence. "Here, doggy! Here, Killer!" Lucy called. "Lucy has yummy apples for you!"

Brian, Bradley, and Nate were still at the knothole. "It worked!" Nate yelled. "Killer's running toward Lucy!"

Bradley and Nate held the ladder while Brian scrambled up. At the top, he looked toward where he could hear Killer gobbling up the apples. Because of the bushes, the dog couldn't see him.

Brian jumped into the neighbors'

yard. "Send the ladder over!" he yelled through the fence.

Bradley and Nate hoisted the ladder up and shoved it. They heard it drop onto the neighbors' lawn.

Bradley stuck his eye to the knot-hole. He saw Brian heading for the blue tarp at the same time that Lucy yelled, "The green car is coming!" She raced toward Bradley and Nate. "Your neighbors are back!"

Bradley put his mouth to the knot-hole and shouted, "Brian, the neighbors are coming! Escape, dude!"

They heard car doors slamming.

They heard Killer barking with happiness.

Just then, the top of the ladder appeared over the fence. Brian came next, practically flying over. He landed on the ground at Bradley's feet.

Brian's face was red, but he was

grinning. "That was close!" he said. He rubbed his arm. "Skinned the heck out of my elbow!"

"But where's your money jar?" Bradley asked his twin. "And my flashlight?"

Brian got up and brushed off his pants. "I didn't have time to get to the tree," he said. "Sorry, bro."

Nate was looking through the knothole. "The car is inside the gate now!" he whispered.

The dog was barking like mad.

"Get Dad's ladder!" Bradley said.

"How?" Brian said. "I can't reach it!" He grabbed his brother's arm and started to run.

The four kids raced into the barn. They flopped down on a pile of hay outside Polly's stall. The pony looked over her stall door and made a funny noise with her lips.

Bradley reached into the stall and

patted Polly on her nose. "Now the neighbors have your money, my flashlight, and Dad's birthday ladder," he said.

"They have something else," Brian added. "I saw about twenty bags of cement piled up behind the blue tarp. And a bunch of long iron pipes."

6
Brian's New Plan

"Cement and iron?" Bradley said. "Maybe they're building a cage for Killer."

"But why would they buy a rope ladder and bike parts?" Lucy asked.

Brian opened his eyes wide and made a zombie face. *"The Killer Dog Mystery!"* he said in a spooky voice.

Bradley tossed some hay at his brother. "You won't think it's so funny when Dad comes out here looking for his new ladder," he said.

Just then, they heard a loud buzzing sound.

"That's coming from their yard!" Bradley said.

"What the heck is that?" Nate asked. "It sounds like an airplane!"

"It's a chain saw," Lucy said. "My dad has one. He uses it to cut down trees."

"Oh no!" Brian said. "How will we get our things back if they cut the tree down?"

Five minutes later, the buzzing noise stopped. The kids ran back to the fence. Lucy got to the knothole first. "I can see the tarp and the dog," she said. "No people. No chain saw."

"We need a plan," Brian said.

"We *had* a plan," Bradley said.

"And it would have worked if the neighbors hadn't come back so soon," Brian said.

"And if their dog wasn't a giant monster!" Bradley said.

"In the movies, the burglars feed the guard dogs sleeping pills," Nate said. "When they fall asleep, the burglars walk right past them!"

Brian grinned. "We don't have sleeping pills," he said. "But you gave me an awesome idea, Nate. I can sneak over there when the Sargents and Killer are asleep!"

"How are you going to get over the fence?" Bradley asked. "Dad's ladder is still on their side, remember? And the gate will be locked."

"Easy," Brian said. "You three will boost me over. Then I'll unlatch the gate, and you guys can come in. We'll grab Dad's ladder and my money jar and run back home. Cinchy!"

"And my flashlight!" Bradley said.

"It will be in the papers tomorrow," Nate said. He closed his eyes and said, "Killer Dog Eats Redheaded Boy."

"Not to worry," Brian said. "I can outrun that big old dog."

"I like your plan," Lucy said. "When can we do it?"

"How about Wednesday night?" Brian said. "Your families are all coming to our house. We'll get permission for you guys to sleep over. At midnight, we'll sneak out. It'll be fun!"

Nate opened his eyes wide. "Creeping around in the dark with a killer dog on the loose doesn't sound like fun!" he said.

Brian stood. "Operation Brian is a perfect plan," he said. "Nothing will go wrong."

Bradley laughed. "Gee, sneaking past Mom and Dad's bedroom, climbing over a fence in the dark, fighting off a monster dog—what could possibly go wrong?"

Brian grinned. "Trust me," he said.

During school recess the next day, the four kids talked about Operation Brian.

"We should all wear dark clothes," Brian said. "Like ninjas."

"I still think it's crazy," Nate said. "That dog is gigantic!"

"I sure hope Mom and Dad don't wake up and catch us," Bradley said.

The next day was Wednesday. Nate's family came to Bradley's house for dinner at six-thirty. Lucy and Dink's family showed up a few minutes later. Nate and Lucy had permission to sleep over. They each brought a sleeping bag. Hidden inside the sleeping bags were their dark clothes.

Thirteen people sat down to eat supper. Dink, Josh, and Ruth Rose were excited about Thanksgiving the next day.

Bradley, Brian, Nate, and Lucy were excited about Operation Brian. It was only five hours away.

After supper, everyone played board games. The kids played Scrabble. Nate went first, and he made DOG as his word.

"Did you see our new neighbors' dog?" Josh asked Dink and Ruth Rose. "He's the biggest monster I've ever seen!"

Bradley poked Brian, Nate, and Lucy under the table. They all grinned.

At ten o'clock, the Duncans and Hathaways thanked the Pintos for supper and went home. Nate and Lucy followed the twins upstairs to their room and unrolled their sleeping bags under the window.

Next door, the tarp glowed from the light inside.

The kids saw shapes moving around behind the tarp.

They heard sanding noises and scraping noises and hammering noises and chain-saw noises.

They heard Mr. and Mrs. Sargent laughing.

"They're working on their secret project," Lucy said.

"What could it be?" Nate asked.

"We'll know pretty soon," Brian said.

"If your plan works," Nate said.

"Operation Brian will totally work," Brian declared. "In two hours, we'll know what's going on inside that blue tarp. And we'll have Dad's ladder, my money, and Bradley's flashlight."

Their dad's voice came from downstairs: "Go to sleep! Not a peep! Or up the stairs I'll creep!"

Lucy giggled. "Your dad is so funny!"

"Not if he catches us sneaking out," Bradley said.

The four kids pulled on their dark clothes.

The twins got into their beds, and Nate and Lucy crawled into their sleeping bags.

Bradley shut off the light.

"How will we know when it's midnight?" Nate asked.

"I'll wake you," Brian said. "I've got the clock in bed with me so Mom, Dad, and Josh won't hear the alarm. I set it for twelve o'clock."

"This will be so exciting!" Lucy said. "I've never snuck out in the middle of the night before!"

7
Operation Brian

Bradley woke up to more strange noises. He turned to look at his clock. It was gone. Then he remembered that Brian had it in his bed.

Bradley heard car doors slamming. He heard people talking outside. It sounded like more than two people, and they were giggling. Who would be laughing outside in the dark? he wondered.

Then Bradley heard a dog barking. It was a big bark from a big dog. *What's Killer the dog doing outside in the mid-*

dle of the night? Bradley wondered. *If Killer sleeps outdoors tonight, Brian's plan is doomed!*

That was Bradley's last thought before he went back to sleep.

Suddenly he heard a soft ringing noise. Ten seconds later, something grabbed his arm. He lunged up and yelled, "AHHHH!"

"Quiet—you'll wake Mom and Dad!" Brian whispered. "Come on. It's time for OB."

"What's OB?" Nate asked from his sleeping bag.

"Operation Brian!" Brian whispered. "Get up."

"Is it midnight already?" Lucy asked. She crawled out of her sleeping bag. Yawning, she pushed her long blond hair out of her eyes.

The kids tugged on their sneakers in the dark.

"Brian, I heard their dog barking," Bradley whispered. "I think Killer is outside!"

Brian looked at Bradley. "When did you hear him?" he asked. "He's not barking now."

"A while ago," Bradley said. "When I was sleeping, but I woke up, I think."

Brian grinned. "You were having one

of your famous nightmares," he said. "You guys ready? Come on!"

With Brian leading, they tiptoed down the hall.

They went past Brian and Bradley's parents' room, then the bathroom. They passed Josh's room. Bradley noticed light under his door. *Why is Josh still awake?* he wondered.

They went down the stairs.

Through the kitchen, where Brian grabbed another apple.

Out the door.

Operation Brian was working!

The kids crept across the backyard. The moon was nearly full, lighting the way to the fence. Their sneakers made no sounds on the soft grass.

Bradley put his eye to the knothole. "Nothing moving," he reported.

"Can you see Killer?" Brian asked.

Bradley looked again. "Nope, just the big blue tarp," he said. "But he could be out there somewhere."

"That's why I brought this," Brian said. He tossed the apple over the fence, then put his eye to the knothole. "No noise, no dog. So now you guys can boost me up, like they do in the Boy Scouts."

"I'm not a Boy Scout," Lucy said.

"I'm not even a Cub Scout," Nate added.

"Josh taught me this," Brian said. He told Nate and Lucy to squat down. He showed them how to make a seat by crisscrossing their hands and arms. When they were ready, Brian put one foot on top of their joined hands. He balanced by holding on to Bradley's head.

Nate and Lucy stood up, slowly lifting Brian.

"You're heavy," Nate grunted.

"You're pulling my hair!" Bradley said.

Brian grabbed the top of the fence. "A little higher!" he said.

Bradley shoved his brother's rear end.

"Okay, I'm up!" Brian said. "Go to the gate, and I'll let you in!"

"Unless Killer eats you first!" Nate said.

Brian grinned in the moonlight. "Killer is in the house dreaming doggy dreams," he said. Then he dropped out

of sight into the neighbors' yard.

Bradley, Nate, and Lucy raced toward the gate.

When they got there, Brian was shoving it open. "Come on in," he whispered. "And be quiet!"

Single file, they followed Brian across the yard. In the moonlight, the tarp was a tall blue ghost. The green car sat in the driveway. Bradley thought it looked like a crouching dragon. Moonlight made the car's headlights gleam like eyes.

Suddenly the house lit up.

A light went on inside the tarp.

The yard was filled with bright light, as if it were noon instead of midnight. Then the neighbors' back door opened. Killer came bounding out, barking like crazy.

He charged across the yard, straight toward Bradley.

8
Surprise!

Killer barked like a maniac. His eyes and teeth shone in the moonlight. He reared up on his hind legs and slammed his giant front paws into Bradley's chest.

My nightmare is coming true! Bradley thought as he landed on his back on the grass. One hundred pounds of hairy black dog piled on top of him. A huge pink tongue washed his face. Bradley was too scared to yell.

"Daisy, get off!" a voice shouted.

Bradley looked up. He saw a boy tugging on the dog's collar. Then a girl was there, and she was tugging, too. They both had brown hair. They looked about ten years old.

Finally, Daisy got off, and Bradley looked up. Brian, Nate, and Lucy were standing with Bradley's parents, who were wearing bathrobes. Josh was there, too, wearing sweatpants, a hoodie, and a silly grin.

Suddenly Pal raced through the gate, into the crowd. He and Daisy sniffed each other, then began racing around the yard, playing doggy tag.

"What're you guys doing here?" Bradley asked his family.

"A better question," his dad said, "is what are *you* doing here?"

Josh helped Bradley up off the ground. The two new kids were standing next to the neighbors.

"These are our grandchildren from

Florida," Mrs. Sargent said. "Charlie and Maddy."

Everyone said hi.

"It's cold out here," Mr. Sargent said. "Let's go inside."

Eleven people crowded into the neighbors' kitchen.

"Find your seat, everyone," Mrs. Sargent said. "The hot chocolate is almost ready."

Bradley blinked under a bright light. A long table was set with eleven places. There were eleven mugs, eleven napkins, eleven spoons. A plate of cookies sat in the middle of the table. The cookies were shaped like turkeys, with raisins for eyes.

On each place mat was a cardboard-turkey name tag. Bradley found his name and sat down. Then he laughed. Standing next to his mug was his flashlight!

Next to him, Brian laughed, too.
There was his jar of money.

They knew we were coming! Bradley
said to himself.

Soon everyone began sipping from

the mugs and munching on cookies.

"How did you know about Operation Brian?" Brian asked.

"A little birdie told us," Mr. Sargent said. "So we knew you were curious about what was going on under our tarp."

"The same little birdie told us your plan about sneaking over here tonight," Bradley's mother said.

"What little birdie?" Bradley asked.

Josh grinned and patted himself on the chest. "Tweet, tweet!" he said. "I heard you guys talking in your room. You should keep your door closed!"

"We had fun sitting in the dark and watching you sneak into the yard," Mrs. Sargent said.

"And I heard you creeping past my door," Josh said. "You were about as quiet as a herd of elephants!"

"So I nearly broke my neck for nothing!" Brian said.

"And I got attacked by a giant dog for nothing!" Bradley said.

"Daisy wouldn't hurt a fly," Maddy said. "She just wanted to kiss you."

"If you had asked, we would have told you," Mrs. Sargent said. "We're building a special Thanksgiving surprise for Charlie and Maddy."

"Granddad, what is it?" Charlie asked. "I can't wait till tomorrow!"

Mr. Sargent stood up and looked at his watch. "Well, since it's almost one in the morning, it's officially Thanksgiving Day," he said. "Let's go take a look!"

Charlie and Maddy raced out the door. Bradley, Brian, Nate, and Lucy ran after them.

Everyone gathered in front of the blue tarp. Mrs. Sargent tugged on a rope, and the tarp fell to the ground.

The "surprise" was tall and silver and shiny. It gleamed in the moonlight.

"It's a space shuttle!" Maddy shouted.

"Thank you, Grandpa and Grandma!"

"Charlie and Maddy live near the Kennedy Space Center in Florida," Mrs. Sargent explained. "They love to go there and see the launches. So we decided to build them their own shuttle in our backyard!"

"But where's the tree?" Bradley asked.

"It's inside," Mr. Sargent said. "We cut off most of the branches and used some of the wood inside the shuttle. The tree is very old, so we used cement and steel bars to make it stronger."

The spaceship was made of aluminum that covered the tree, and light shone through round windows. There was a door to go inside.

"It's wonderful!" Bradley's mother said. "What clever new neighbors we have!"

"Can we go in it?" Nate asked.

"Of course," Mr. Sargent said.

The kids opened the door and stepped inside, where Bradley and Brian used to play. The wood from the tree branches had been turned into seats. A rope ladder hung from the top. One by one, the kids climbed the ladder. It led to a platform where they could sit on pillows.

Sticking up from the floor were a bike seat and two pedals attached to a chain. The chain was hooked up to a small motor.

Charlie sat on the bike seat, put his feet on the pedals, and pushed down. Suddenly one of the windows turned into a TV screen. At first, it was black, but then the kids saw planets and stars appear.

"Awesome!" Nate said. "I feel like an astronaut!"

9
Thanksgiving Friends

Everyone got a chance to go inside the space shuttle. Finally, the kids began to yawn. "Okay, it's time to call it a night," Bradley's father said. "Happy Thanksgiving, everyone!"

Bradley, Brian, Nate, and Lucy went back to the twins' room. Within minutes, they were all asleep.

On Thanksgiving morning, a loud barking woke Bradley. He crawled over Nate's sleeping bag and looked down at the ground. On the other side of the fence, Daisy was barking. Pal was sitting on his side of the fence, barking right back!

Brian woke up and looked out the window.

Mr. Pinto and Mr. Sargent were standing by the fence, talking. Mr. Sargent was holding his chain saw.

Nate sat up. "What's going on?" he asked.

"My dad and Mr. Sargent are out there talking," Bradley said.

Lucy's head popped up. She rested her chin on the sill and looked down.

Suddenly Mr. Sargent started the chain saw. He began cutting the fence. In two minutes, there was a big space where a section of the fence had fallen to the ground.

Pal raced into the Sargents' yard. He and Daisy began chasing each other.

"Oh my gosh, there's a big hole in the fence!" Bradley said.

"Charlie and Maddy are already playing in the shuttle!" Brian said.

The four kids ran downstairs and dashed outside. Charlie and Maddy waved to them. "Come on up!" they yelled.

The cutout section of fence was lying on the grass. Mr. Sargent was measuring it with his shiny tape. "I can make a nifty gate out of this wood," he said.

"I think I've got some hinges in the barn," Bradley's father said.

"What're you doing, Dad?" Bradley asked his father.

"Our new neighbor decided there should be a gate here," Mr. Pinto said.

Mr. Sargent smiled. "Our grandkids will be leaving soon, and we want *you* kids to play in the space shuttle while they're gone," he said. "The gate will always be unlocked for you."

Mrs. Sargent poked her head out the back door. "What's all the racket?" she asked.

"Grandpa cut part of the fence down!" Charlie said.

"Oh, what a marvelous idea!" Mrs. Sargent said. "Now it will be so much easier to get to know our new friends!"

Bradley's mother opened her back door. "Everyone come over for juice and muffins!" she called across the yard.

Charlie and Maddy came down, and they all walked through the hole where the fence once stood.

Bradley whispered to his mother, "Mom, can we invite everyone over for Thanksgiving dinner?"

His mother smiled. "I already asked them," she whispered back. "Now I just have to figure out where to get a bigger table!"

If you like Calendar Mysteries,
you might want to read
A to Z Mysteries!
Help Dink, Josh, and Ruth Rose . . .

. . . solve mysteries from A to Z!

The Adventures of Hector Fuller

BOOK 4

Hector on Thin Ice

By Elizabeth Shreeve
Illustrated by Pamela R. Levy

ALADDIN PAPERBACKS
New York London Toronto Sydney

To David, James, and Sam

First Aladdin Paperbacks edition September 2004

Text copyright © 2004 by Elizabeth Shreeve
Illustrations copyright © 2004 by Pamela Levy

ALADDIN PAPERBACKS
An imprint of Simon & Schuster
Children's Publishing Division
1230 Avenue of the Americas
New York, NY 10020

Designed by Debra Sfetsios
The text of this book was set in Graham.

Printed in the United States of America
2 4 6 8 10 9 7 5 3 1
Library of Congress Control Number 2003116540
ISBN 0-689-86417-5

BOOK 4

Hector on Thin Ice

Table of Contents

Chapter One

Rock in a Hard Place

"**I**'ll get you out of there if it's the last thing I do!"

Hector Fuller the wumblebug stomped his six feet and shouted at the wall. A wall of solid rock—except for one soft and crumbly place. And in that place, in that last possible tunnel, was a giant pebble that refused to budge.

This hill seemed perfect, at first. Too high to flood. A view of the garden. Close to friends. Hector dug into the soft earth, dreaming of a kitchen and a quiet bedroom deep underground. Tunnels, storage rooms, and a spot for his piano, the one thing he'd rescued from the autumn flood.

Then he hit rock. No matter where he

scraped and scratched, all he found were the hard bones of the hill. And now this pebble was blocking his last hope. After weeks of work, all he had to show was one small room piled with brown dirt.

Well, the pebble had to move. It *had* to. Winter was coming—time for small creatures to sleep through the cold months, far from snow and ice. And every year, Hector's friends gathered in his hole to celebrate the longest night and say good-bye until spring.

Everyone would come. Everyone would expect Hector to be finished. After all, Hector was a wumblebug, and wumblebugs can dig anything. Anytime.

Hector swung his back legs and kicked the pebble with all his might.

"Yee-owwww!" He sprawled on the ground in pain. The pebble wobbled, rolled forward over Hector's antennae, then slipped back into the tunnel and settled down with a *thunk.*

"Hopeless," muttered Hector. He threw a bit of dirt at the wall and a tiny drift of wind blew it back in his face. There was a tunnel there, all right. And a rock, too big for one wumblebug to move.

Hector turned and limped away, feeling somehow that the pebble was smiling behind his back.

But the pebble's *thunk* kept going, echoing deep inside the hill, into the dreams of creatures already hidden in winter sleep.

Chapter Two

Slippery Slope

Outside Hector's hole, a few snowflakes drifted in the cold, still air. The low winter sun cast shadows over a thin layer of white snow.

Hector shivered and took a step. *Whoosh!* His legs slipped on a patch of ice. *Whish!* He flipped onto his back and slid down the hill, faster and faster, his legs wiggling and his whole body spinning in circles as he tumbled into a snowdrift at the bottom of the slope.

Ker-lumph! A sled zoomed down the hill behind Hector and crashed next to him. *Flump! Flump!* The sled burst into pieces. Hector's favorite cousin, Suzy the ladybug, fell off to one side. His best friend, Lance the lacewing, flopped off on the other. Both of them rolled in the snow and laughed.

"Hector!" said Suzy. "You've got to take a ride!"

"On what?" said Hector.

"The sled, of course!" Lance stood up and looked at the remains of the sled—two pine needles and a scrap of bark. "Whoops. Oh well—we'll put it together again."

"No thanks," said Hector. "It's cold enough without diving headfirst into snow. How are the honeybees?"

"Sealed in the hive and tucked in tight," said Lance. "My work's done for the year. How about you? How's the digging going?"

"To tell you the truth . . . it's slow. I'm finding lots of rock."

"Don't worry, Hector. If anybody can do it, you can," said Lance. "Any neighbors yet?"

Hector shook his head.

"That's good," said Suzy, brushing the snow

off her spots. "From what I hear, that hill is full of caves. And somebody said there used to be ant lions in some of them. Ant lions will eat anything in the winter. Even red bugs."

"I haven't seen any," said Hector. "They must have been washed away in the flood, like us."

Suzy looked down at Hector, still slumped in the snowdrift. "You know, we could skip the party this year. There's only a few days left."

"Skip the party? Not a chance!" Lance waved his long antennae. "What would winter be without a party at Hector's house? Party or bust, party we must! Even if we need to do it out here in the snow."

"I'll be ready," said Hector. He stood up and fluttered his short wings. "Somehow or other, I'll get it done."

"You bet!" said Lance. "We'll have a party— the big one!"

"Maybe bigger than we thought," said Suzy. "Looks like we've got company."

Chapter Three

Over the Snow

"Hi! Hello!" came some voices. "We're here!"

Hector and his friends looked up and stared.

Alongside the stream came a sleigh, made from a seashell and pulled by a centipede whose many legs rippled over the snow. The sleigh was bursting with wumblebugs—two big bugs holding the reins and a crowd of wumblepups in the back, all waving and shouting at the same time.

"Hector, Uncle Hector, we're here!" they yelled as the centipede turned from the stream and pulled the sleigh up through the garden toward the hill.

"Who is it?" whispered Suzy.

"Looks like my brother, Cosmo," answered Hector, his eyes wide. "And his wife. And their pups . . . looks like three. No, four. No . . . looks like . . ."

"Looks like too many to count," said Lance. "Did you know they were coming?"

"Believe me," said Hector. "I had no idea."

The sleigh pulled up, the centipede collapsed on the ground, and Hector's brother jumped down and tackled him in a painful hug.

"Hector, old bug! Long time no see! It's good to be home!"

"Home?" said Hector. "But—"

"You remember Mamie, don't you?" Cosmo pointed to the sleigh, and Hector's sister-in-law waved from the back where two of the boy pups were wrestling and another was dangling off the side. "Come on, everybody. Show your faces! There we are—Sophie, our eldest, and Otis and Oscar and Lulu and BK and Globug and Gin. And a few more . . ." he waved at a

pile of unborn wumblepups still tucked inside their cocoons ". . . but we don't have names for them yet. Any day now!"

Hector's mouth dropped open as the wumble-pups jumped and fluttered from the sleigh and grabbed him in another tight squeeze.

"Oh, Uncle Hector!" cried one of the pups. "Isn't it great? Mama and Pop say we can stay as long as we want!"

"The minute it snowed, we jumped in the sleigh and here we are!" said a second pup.

"Our house got ruined in the flood . . ." said a third.

"So Pop says we'll live here all winter with you!" finished a fourth.

Hector tried to find his voice. "Wh . . . wh . . . what a surprise! But . . . you've come to stay . . ." he stammered, "stay where?"

"Oh, Hector, you old joker," said Cosmo, giving him a friendly punch. "We're staying with you, of course."

Chapter Four

Lulu

"There's no room!" cried Hector. "I've only started digging! It's only a tiny, rough, little—"

"Aren't you happy to see us, Uncle Hector?" said a small voice. Hector looked down at one of the girl pups, who looked up with wide eyes.

"Well, yes," answered Hector. "It's just that—"

"Now, Lulu," said Cosmo. "Sure he's happy, right, old bug?" Cosmo jumped back onto the sleigh and began dropping bundles for Hector to catch. "Here, let's unload. Not too heavy for you, is it?"

"No, but—"

"That reminds me of a joke." Cosmo stopped in mid-throw, and his face grew serious.

"No!" said Hector. "No jokes, please. Anything but—"

"Tell me, brother," Cosmo went on. "What weighs more—an ounce of thistledown or an ounce of rocks?"

"Well, I suppose . . . oh, for heaven's sake. They weigh the same, of course."

Lance laughed. "Hey, Hector, aren't you going to introduce us?"

"Uh . . . sure," said Hector. His head spun as wumblepups jumped everywhere and Cosmo threw more packages down from the sleigh. "This is Cosmo, my brother, and Mamie, his wife. And here's my friend, Lance, and you know Cousin Suzy."

"Cousin ladybug, of course," said Cosmo, looking serious again. "So, anyway, why did the ladybug cross the road?"

"Let's see," said Suzy. "Maybe she—"

"Wrong," said Cosmo. "She spotted something to wear! Ha-ha!"

"Good one!" said Lance. "Okay, so where do you find a turtle without any legs?"

"Hmm," said Cosmo. "Maybe . . . under a rock?"

"No." Lance grinned. "Right where you left her!"

"Here we go again," muttered Hector as everyone laughed. Then he felt a slight tug and looked down to see Lulu standing by his side.

"Is it true, what they say?" she whispered, her short antennae twisting and curling as she spoke. "Did you really fall into the honey?"

"What? Oh, at the bee farm? Well, yes. In fact—"

"Was it sweet? Did you taste it? Did you like it?"

"Definitely sweet. But—"

"Yum! Was it sticky? Could you swim?"

"Not very well. Actually—"

"How long did you swim? Are you a good

swimmer? What would have happened if the bees didn't pull you out?"

"If they . . . well, I guess that would have been the end."

Lulu sighed. "You're so brave, Uncle Hector. When I'm big, I want to be an adventurer like you."

Hector stood still, watching Lance lead Cosmo's family up the hill, watching Suzy wave good-bye, and watching the centipede wriggle off along the edge of the icy stream. Adventure seemed far away. "Let's go," he said to Lulu, and bent down to pick up some more bags left on the ground.

"Uncle Hector, do you see? Do you see?" Lulu pointed to a tree that had lost its leaves for winter and now was full of butterflies. Every dark branch quivered with their fluttering orange wings.

One of the butterflies circled over Hector's head.

"Good-bye!" Hector called and waved. The butterfly circled again and the entire flock rose up, filling the winter sky with a cloud of color as the butterflies caught the winds that would carry them to a warmer place.

"Uncle Hector," said Lulu, "do you know why butterflies fly south for the winter?"

"Certainly," said Hector. "They need to . . ."

Lulu smiled a tiny smile and leaned against Hector's wing. "No, no," she said. "Because it's too far to walk."

Chapter Five

Chaos

Back in Hector's small cave, heaps of food and luggage lay everywhere. Wumblepups jumped on the bed and slid down piles of dirt, spreading it over the floor and filling the air with dust. The snow from their many feet melted in puddles and turned the floor into mud.

"My, my!" said Mamie. "This will be cozy!"

"Now do you see what I mean?" asked Hector. "I'm sorry to say that—"

"Don't apologize! Now let's see . . . where can I put these babies that they'll be safe?" Mamie looked around the cave, her arms full of cocoons.

"Mama, I'm hungry!" called Globug, one of the smallest girl pups.

"Me, too," said BK, one of the boys. "Pop, let's

make us a fire and heat lotsa honeysuckle, 'kay?"

"You go ahead," said Cosmo. "Hey, Hector, what happened to all your stuff?"

"Washed away in the flood," said Hector. "I lost everything—my furniture, my books . . ."

Cosmo's antennae drooped. "Your books— that's too bad. But it reminds me . . . what do you do when a termite chews on your book?"

"Wait, wait," said Lance. "I'll think of it. Maybe . . ."

"You take the words right out of his mouth!" said Cosmo.

Lance bent his long body back in a laugh. "Ha! Okay, how about this—what kind of books do skunks read?"

"Best smellers?" offered Lulu with a grin. She stood by a small, smoking fire that the pups had started in the middle of the room.

"You got it!" Lance said and coughed. "Phew—time to go. Cheer up, Hector. Just think—more guests for the party!"

"More guests," muttered Hector as Lance slipped out. "More chaos. More noise. More—"

"I've got it!" said Mamie. "I'll put them in here." She lifted the top of Hector's piano and placed the cocoons inside. "There, my little chrysalises. Have a good sleep!"

"Not the piano!" Hector protested. "It's—"

"Don't worry . . . they'll love the music. What do you think, pups? Shall Uncle Hector play us a song?"

"Play! Play!" yelled the wumblepups. "Let's play a song!" They ran to the piano and began to pound the keys, dripping sticky nectar and covering the pedals with mud.

Smoke filled the room as the pups shouted and sang.

Mamie and Cosmo hurried about, unpacking and setting up beds.

And no seemed to notice when Hector turned away and slipped out the door.

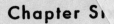

Snowflakes

Cold air hit Hector like a wall. He hurried from the crowded cave without looking or thinking. He wanted to be alone—alone in the big, quiet night. His family would not mind. They had come to him for shelter and now they were safe and warm and busy inside.

A shadow fell over Hector's path—something flying by overhead. Who would be flying on a cold night like this?

An owl. Owls can see everything, even in the dark. Would an owl bother to hunt for a wumblebug, a small beetle that didn't even taste good?

Hector did not wait to find out.

He sped across the snow. The owl's shadow

23

followed him, its tufts of feathers like horns. He hurtled under a bush. The bird swooped by again. He tripped and fell among the roots and stems, knocking off clumps of snow. Hector tumbled into a ditch and the clumps poured over him, burying him upside down in a thick white layer. The owl flew away.

No problem, thought Hector. *I can dig myself out.* He pushed the snow aside with his front legs. More snow took its place. He pushed harder with four legs this time, but the powder fell back and covered him up. He dug faster, kicking all his legs and flapping his wings, until he could see a piece of the sky.

What a sight! The moon peeked out between the clouds and snowflakes fell like tiny, wet stars. Each crystal had six points but each one was different—some rounded, some sharp like the leaves of a fern. Hector lay on his back and counted—five, ten, twenty-five snowflakes falling . . . drifting . . . gliding down through the

air. Together, they coated the ground with a smooth blanket that covered all the bumps and soaked up all the sounds.

"Don't move," Hector whispered to no one but himself. He stopped digging and stared up at the sky. Just for a few minutes, he would be quiet and calm.

No noise and confusion.

No bad jokes.

He would stay still and watch the snow fall. What was wrong with that?

Chapter Seven

Wumblepups to
the Rescue

"Uncle Hector? Is that you?"

Hector opened one eye, then another. He blinked back the snow and saw Lulu and BK standing at the top of the ditch.

"What are you doing?" called Lulu. "Mama says you must come inside!"

"Mmm," said Hector. "Go away."

"You better ssthnap out of it!" BK shook a leg. "You feeze to deaf out here!"

"He's right," said Lulu. "Your antennae will freeze. What would happen then? Do you think they would break off?"

"Don't know," answered Hector. His mouth was stiff from the cold. "Don't care."

The snow was falling harder now. Lulu

danced on the edge of the ditch, dodging the snowflakes. BK dodged them, too. "Look, Uncle Hector! Can you see what we're doing? Want to try?"

Hector closed his eyes again. Dodging snowflakes was too much work.

"Okay, we're coming down!" cried Lulu, and she and BK slid into the ditch, yelling and screeching and landing with a *flump*. "Wow, that's fun! But how'll we get out? Can you help us, Uncle Hector? Can you?"

"I'm busy," Hector murmured. "Counting snow."

"You 'bout to feeze!" said BK.

"He's right again," said Lulu. "Come on, Uncle Hector. You've got to get up, like it or not. Stand here, BK, and when I say . . . ready or not . . . *umph!*" The two wumblepups squeezed behind Hector and pushed him up onto his feet.

"Mmm." Hector shivered and sat down. He

felt heavy and cold, as if he were trapped under a mountain of ice.

Lulu stared her uncle straight in the eye.

"Do you know everybody's looking for you? Every wumblebug in your whole family is out in the snow where no bug should ever, ever be. Maybe they're frozen and maybe they're lost and all you can say is *'mmm'*? What kind of answer is that?"

"She's right," said BK. "It's now 'r never, Uncle Hector."

Hector dragged himself up. He trembled. He hurt. He felt that his legs were about to break off.

Lulu shoved him on one side. Hector took a step and almost sat down, but BK jabbed him on the other side and they staggered toward the slope. The two wumblepups got behind Hector and pushed. Scramble-push. Scramble-push-slip-slide. Up the ditch they struggled, until they stood at the top in heavy snow.

All their tracks and paths were swallowed up by white.

"Which way, Uncle Hector? Which way is home?"

Hector bent his antennae up the hill. "We'll go up," he mumbled. "If we go up, we'll find the hole."

"We'll follow you," said Lulu. "And when we get there, we'll tell you our great idea."

Chapter Eight

It Couldn't Be Done

The smallest wumblebugs jumped up when Hector staggered into the cave, followed by Lulu and BK.

"You found him!" they cried, and ran outside to announce the news. "Come back, everybody! Uncle Hector's here!"

Hector flopped down. The room was just as crowded as he remembered, but the fire was warm and Cosmo had made a chimney from a long hollow stem. The floor was covered with dry leaves. A painting of an elderly wumblelady leaned against one wall.

"Grandma!" sighed Hector. "You found my grandma!"

"Our grandma, right?" said Lulu. "We found

her when we were looking around for you. There's lots of stuff around here, don't you know?"

They heard voices outside and then one by one the wumblebugs appeared at the tunnel. Each one lugged something into the room.

"There you go, brother." Cosmo set a big, soft chair down by the fire and motioned for Hector to sit.

"My chair!" cried Hector.

"And I found these." Sophie dropped a pile of books at Hector's feet.

"My books!"

"And this." Oscar struggled in with a piano bench, missing one leg.

"And look what Mama found!" yelled Globug and Gin, balancing a teapot, two broken cups, and one saucer. "We'll have a tea party!"

"Remember this?" Lulu held up a wrinkled, dirty bag—Hector's backpack. "Isn't it useful,

Uncle Hector? Don't you take it on your trips?"

"My goodness," said Hector. "I haven't been on a trip for a while. I've just been digging. This is . . . this is . . ."

"This is kinda crowded," said BK. "All this stuff. So, you wanna hear the plan? Tell him, Pop."

Hector sat up in the big chair, waiting to hear. The pups waited, too.

"We'll expand," said Cosmo. "We'll dig a new cave to fit everyone."

"Impossible."

"Why?"

Hector waved a leg around the room. "Because that wall is rock . . . and that wall is rock . . . and that one is rock . . . and over there is a pebble that won't move."

"We'll find a new cave."

Hector shook his head. "It's snowing too hard. All the tunnels will be covered up."

"Then," said Mamie, looking up from the cocoons, "we'll move the pebble."

"It won't budge," said Hector. "Believe me, I've pushed and pulled for hours, and—"

"But Uncle Hector," said Lulu. "If we do it together, we'll—"

"You can't."

"We can."

"Let's try," said Cosmo. "Globug and Gin, loosen that edge where it's jammed in tight. BK, Lulu, get the other side clear. Oscar, on that side, there you go . . . Otis, over here. Sophie, next to me."

"C'mon, everybody! We gonna move that pebble, now!" called BK. The wumblepups swarmed around the pebble, scraping and scratching with their small legs.

"Ready?" said Cosmo. "On the count of three. One . . . two . . ." the wumblebugs chanted together.

"Wait!" cried Hector. "You'll just push it deeper down the tunnel. There might be someone asleep down there. Like maybe a—"

"Three!" they yelled. *Pop!* The pebble burst loose, hit the side of the tunnel with a *thud,* and bumped its way down into the hill, into rooms and halls and places they could not see. *THUMP-THUMP-thump-bump-bump-bum-bum-bum-bum.*

"Yippee! We did it!" yelled the pups. "Hurrah!"

"I think," Lulu whispered to Hector, "you must have loosened it up, with all your work, right?"

"Unca Hector, will ya play the piano now?" said BK.

"Play! Play!" yelled the pups, and dragged Hector to the old piano.

Hector sat on the wobbly bench. He felt the keys—a little sticky. He played a few notes—way out of tune. "What about the cocoons?" he asked.

"They'll love it," said Cosmo. "You know what they say. . . ."

Before his brother could say anything else, Hector began to play. The wumblepups clapped their hands and leaped and sang. Lulu climbed a pile of dirt and danced on the top. Hector played more. He played every song he knew and then he started over again.

And the music and noise traveled into the hill, following the pebble through the tunnels and waking the sleeping creatures huddled in their caves.

One of them looked up and frowned with hunger. He was a large and carnivorous bug, and he was not far away.

Chapter Nine

Bucket Brigade

"You want to build all that?" asked Hector.

The pups nodded and held up a piece of bark for Hector to see. Scratched on the reverse side was a plan for the wumblebug hole—a huge main cave with connecting tunnels and sleeping burrows and secret exits and two kitchens and places to store food.

"This'll be yours, Unca Hector, 'kay?" said BK, pointing to the cave they were in. "Then we gotta dig this tunnel right here, and . . ."

"It'll take months!" Hector sat up, feeling stiff and sore. He'd given his bed to Mamie and slept on the floor. Now the fire was out and the room was cold and damp. Mamie and Cosmo were busy with two newborn pups that had hatched in the night.

"Not months," said Lulu. "Not if we all help. We've got to get ready for the winter party, right?"

"Listen," said Oscar. "First we dig, then we—"

"We'll never get the dirt out of here," said Hector.

Lulu tugged at Hector's wing. "Say one person filled up some kind of bucket with dirt, and . . ."

"And dey passed it to somebody else," said BK, "and den . . ."

"They passed it to somebody, and . . ."

"Enough talking," said Sophie. "Let's find Uncle Hector some breakfast and get to work."

Globug brought Hector the remains of an acorn—an acorn he'd planned to live on for weeks, now nibbled to almost nothing by the pups—and they began to dig. Hector worked at the front, testing for rock and changing plans as they went. The tunnel grew and the acorn, now loaded with dirt, was handed from Sophie to Otis to Oscar and on down the line to Lulu and BK, who tipped it into the snow. Then Globug and Gin scampered back with the empty nutshell.

Dig! Run! Dig! Run! A cloud of dust filled the cave as the pups moved in a steady rhythm. Cosmo took a place in the line and the pace picked up. They dug a bedroom for Hector and a short tunnel to a softer, sandier place where they dug the big cave. Next came the kitchen with a chimney and a lookout hole and a passage to let rainwater in. All day they worked, pushing the earth aside—more earth than Hector could have dug in months, alone. All that was left was the entry tunnel that would lead to a new front door.

Suddenly Hector held up one leg. "Quiet!" he said to the pups.

"What is it?" asked Cosmo.

"I'm not sure." Hector listened hard. Did he hear something breathing somewhere? "But I think we might be about to break through to . . ."

"To what?" whispered Lulu, her eyes open wide.

"To somebody else's home. A hill like this is sure to be full of tunnels . . . holes . . . homes for bugs. And others, too. Most will be asleep at this time of year. But some of them . . ." Hector turned to Cosmo. "Tell you what—take the pups outside and go sledding or something, so I can think. We might need to change direction for the entry tunnel."

"Outside!" yelled the pups. "Sledding!"

"And stay away from the stream!" Hector called after them. "The ice is still thin."

The pups galloped out—all except Lulu. "What is it, Uncle Hector?" she asked.

Hector shook his head. "I'm not sure. I've got a feeling . . . I think we'd better leave this

tunnel"—he pointed down the path they'd been working on—"and find a new one. What I need is something sharp to scrape with and get through this tight spot."

Lulu dashed back to the cave and returned with a blackberry thorn.

"Perfect!" said Hector. "Now let's see if I can . . ."

Hector turned his back to Lulu and began to probe for a safer route. "Ah!" he said at last, and turned to smile at her.

But Lulu was gone. Her tracks led down the tunnel—the tunnel that led toward the sound of someone breathing through the wall.

Chapter Ten

Deep Sleepers

Hector threw down the thorn and ran after Lulu's tiny footprints. He sniffed the air, full of strange smells. He waved his antennae in circles, searching for her.

The tunnel branched, then branched again and again, becoming wider every time. *Wide enough for something huge,* Hector thought. *Huge and hungry and . . .*

Hector turned a corner and froze. He was in an enormous cavern with a roof as tall as the sky. A trickle of light filtered in from the other side—a world away—so that Hector could see that the ceiling was covered with bodies. Bodies hanging upside down.

"Lulu?" called Hector in a soft voice. There

was no answer, from Lulu or anyone else. He took a step, looking up to see if the creatures overhead would wake up. They didn't move. They barely seemed to breathe. They slept, wrapped in what looked like wings and clinging to the ceiling with hooks on their wings and toes.

"Bats," said Hector. "They've got to be bats." He flew into the air, looking for Lulu's tracks across the floor. She must have flown, too, because her trail disappeared. Then Hector saw a small footprint next to another entrance. He took one last look at the bats sleeping the winter away in their cool, dark cave, and plunged into a new tunnel.

This one smelled strange, too. More like . . . *Food*, thought Hector. *Smells like food.* Suddenly he was very hungry. He went faster, almost forgetting about Lulu's tracks. But Lulu must have done the same thing, because her footprints led Hector straight into somebody's nest.

Oh, the food! A mountain of seeds and grain, acorns and dried-up fruits. More food than Hector had ever imagined—more than a wumblebug could eat in a hundred winters. And perched on top in a bed of grass and hair and leaves was a mouse, curled in a tight little ball with its tail wrapped all the way around and its long back feet sticking out.

I wonder . . . , Hector asked himself, *does a mouse sleep as soundly as a bat?* He pulled a seed from the nest and gobbled it down. Good . . . but not enough. He ate another and then reached for a dried berry, and some more seeds. A whole bunch this time.

With the last seed, the tall nest shifted and slumped and collapsed on one side. "Uurrrugle . . ." growled the mouse in her sleep. She opened one eye, looked straight at Hector, and bared her strong teeth.

Hector dropped the food and ran. Out of the burrow and down another tunnel, not stopping to look for tracks. Down farther he ran, past more branching tunnels and caves carved into the hill, past ants guarding their storerooms of food and termites guarding their queen. He ran in what felt like circles, following his feet, so that when the tunnel ended he was moving too fast to stop. Instead he crashed into a small wumblebug standing at the edge of a cliff, sending them both tumbling into another cave.

A cave full of snakes.

Chapter Eleven

Sleds

"Aaaah!" cried Hector as he slipped down the steep slope.

"Whee!" yelled Lulu as she fell, too.

Plop! Thlump! They landed on the snakes, coiled in a twisted mass that spread out across the entire cave.

"Fly!" cried Hector. "Fly away!" He fluttered his wings, but Lulu stood up and looked around with a smile on her face.

"Aren't they beautiful?" she said. "See their colors? See their stripes? Are they awake? Are they—"

"They're snakes, Lulu. Quick, let's go!"

"I think they're asleep." Lulu crept along the back of a snake and peered into its face. "Do

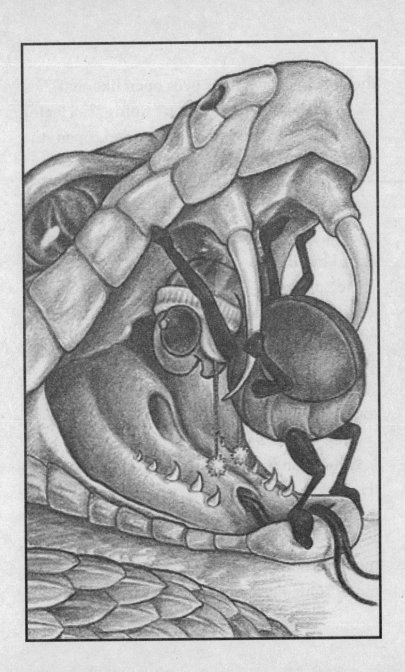

they always have their eyes open like that?"

"What? What are you doing?" Hector watched, horrified, as Lulu pried open the mouth of a snake and peered inside.

"No big deal, Uncle Hector. These guys are asleep. See?" Lulu jumped to another snake and danced on top of its head. It looked blankly ahead but did not move.

Hector took a deep breath. "Yes, they're asleep. Lucky for us, they'll stay half-frozen all winter. We hope. And yes, their eyes are open all the time. They've got no eyelids."

"That's cool. Super-cool. Just like the bats— did you see 'em?"

"Yes. But let's get out of here."

"One more thing." Lulu tugged at a scale on the snake's long back. "These'll make . . ." Lulu grunted as she pulled harder "great . . . sleds!" *Pop!* Lulu tumbled back, clutching the scale, then bounced up and began to peel off some more. "One more for BK. And for Sophie, Otis,

Oscar . . . Perfect!" she said, so loaded down she could barely walk. "Perfect for sledding!"

"Sledding?" said Hector. "For heaven's sake! Here, at least let me carry them." Hector tucked the scales under his front legs. Maybe Lulu was right—the scales were strong and light, with ridges down the centers that would make them go straight and fast through the snow. Hector leaned over and peeled one last scale for himself. "Come on," he said and flew up to the mouth of the tunnel.

Lulu fluttered behind. "Does everybody go to sleep for the winter?" she asked as they hiked back.

"Lots of them fly away."

"Like the butterflies we saw?"

"Yes. And birds, too."

"What about bees? What about bugs?"

Hector sighed. "So many questions! Honeybees go deep in their hive and crowd together to stay warm. As for bugs . . . some go underground, like us, or build a special house inside a leaf. Some make their cocoons at the end of the summer, and then they die. Some spiders, too."

"Oh." Lulu walked for a few moments without speaking. "But what about Cousin Suzy? What about ladybugs?"

"They'll huddle together and sleep inside the bark of a tree."

"Do they sleep for a whole day?"

"Longer."

"Ten days?"

"Longer."

"For . . . for a hundred days?"

"At least. They'll sleep from the start of winter until the snow melts, when the nights aren't so long anymore. Us, too. We'll be so sleepy, you could roll BK across the room and he wouldn't wake up."

Lulu giggled. "I'm gonna stay awake and roll BK across the floor."

They stopped at a fork in the tunnel. Hector

sniffed and stretched his antennae, searching for the right route.

"What's that sound?" said Lulu.

Hector listened hard. Through the wall of the tunnel came the faint *ping-ping* of a piano. And something else, besides. "We can't go that way," he said.

"Why not? The dirt's all loose and sandy here—we should dig a shortcut straight through!"

"No," said Hector. "We need to walk the long way around. This hill is full of strangers."

"Yeah, but they're asleep." Lulu began to scrape at the tunnel wall.

Hector frowned. "I've got a bad feeling about this."

"Relax, Uncle Hector." Lulu broke through into a dark, empty space. "It's an adventure, right? We'll jump through and—"

At that moment the wall blew apart. The tunnel behind them collapsed. And a huge form with barbed pincers and a wide, spiky back burst out of the shadows and reared up over Lulu's head.

The ant lion was awake.

Chapter Twelve

Run for Your Life

"*Y*arrrgh!*" The ant lion lunged at Lulu, ready to snatch her up.

Whack! Without thinking, Hector hit the ant lion with the snake scales, hard enough that the big bug swerved off balance and missed.

"Run!" Hector cried, and bashed the ant lion again. Then he clutched the scales tighter, turned after Lulu, and ran.

What in the world could he do? A wumble-bug was no match for an ant lion—famous for fierceness, famous for gobbling whole families of ants. *Not my family*, thought Hector. *Not mine.* The thought of his family—his whole family— made him run faster than ever before.

Thunk. Behind him, the ant lion was on his

feet. Hector hurtled up the tunnel. He caught a glimpse of Lulu, scurrying ahead. *Thud. Thud.* The ant lion grew closer. The tunnel was starting to look familiar. Hector turned a corner. There was Lulu, gasping for breath and holding the thorn that Hector had been using to dig.

Hector grabbed it and gave her a little push. "Go!" he yelled, and pointed the thorn toward the ant lion as it charged around the corner, its bulky body filling the tunnel around him.

Hector took aim and threw the thorn like a spear at the ant lion's head.

"Uuuurrraaagh!" roared the ant lion and stumbled, long enough for Hector to spin around into the cave where the wumblepups stood and stared.

"Catch!" yelled Hector. He tossed snake scales right and left. "Sophie! Otis! Oscar! Lulu! BK! Globug! Gin! Get going! Get sliding! Get out!"

Lulu led a stampede to the door as the ant

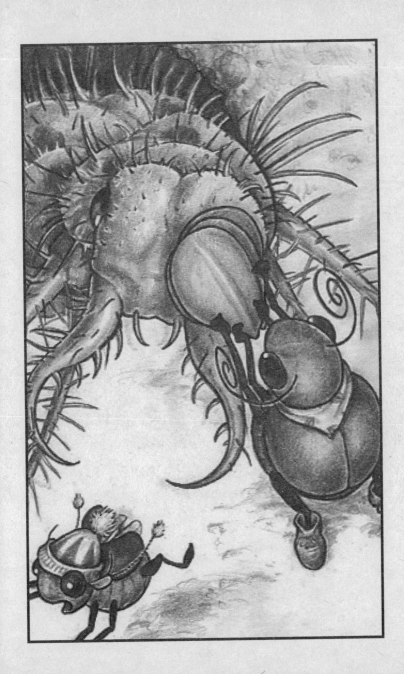

lion stormed into the cave. Hector picked up the picture of his grandmother and hurled it at the ant lion's feet. He threw his big chair. His books. His piano bench.

The ant lion did not slow down. He paid no attention to Hector, standing there in his path. He ignored Cosmo and Mamie, who stood clutching the newborn pups. He crashed through the cave after the wumblepups, who would be juicy and tender to eat.

Chapter Thirteen

Tug-of-War

Hector dashed out the tunnel and leaped onto his snake scale.

Whuuup! The speed took him by surprise. Snow that had melted in the morning sun was refreezing in the afternoon cold, and the surface was slick and fast.

Bump! Bump! Hector held on tight as the sled hit an icy crust. *Shwiiiiishhh!* The noise was terrific. Up ahead, the ant lion lunged toward the wumblepups sliding down the slope, pincers opening and shutting as he tried to catch them.

Hector threw his weight forward and fluttered his wings. *Maybe,* he thought, *if I can get in his way . . .* He shot across the top of the ice.

As he came up to the ant lion, he leaned hard to the right.

"*Raarrgh!*" The ant lion tripped over Hector and flipped tail over pincers, gathering snow, making a bigger and bigger snowball as he fell.

Bump! The ant lion's snowball crashed into Lulu on the way. She slipped from her sled and rolled into a snowball, too. Both snowballs—one big, one small—zoomed down the hill, over the level ground at the bottom, and out onto the thin ice that covered the stream.

Hector steered to the stream bank and hopped off. One by one the pups gathered around and stared.

The ant lion's snowball was beginning to quiver and shake. One barbed pincer poked out, then another.

"Lulu!" shouted BK. "Hurry! Come back!"

Lulu's snowball trembled. One thin leg waved in the air, then stopped.

"We gotta get her," said Globug in a small

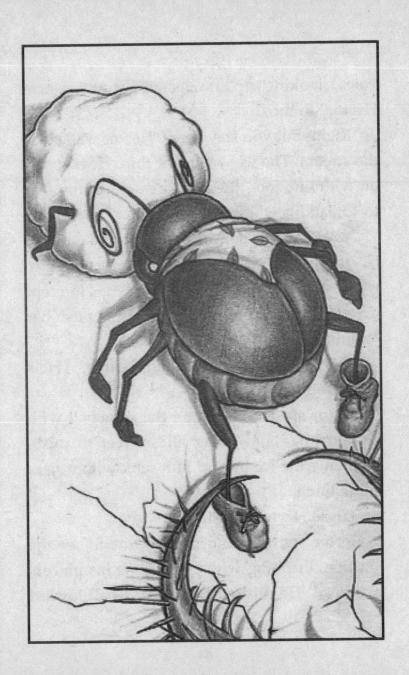

voice, looking up at Hector. "Right, Uncle Hector? Right?"

"Right. But you stay here." Hector walked to the stream. The ice was razor thin. He stepped on with one foot, then another, crouching low to spread his weight.

Creak! Creak! The ice splintered and sagged. Hector made a wide circle around the ant lion, where the ice was already cracked. He crept over to Lulu's snowball and began to push her back to shore.

"Hurry! Hurry!" cried the pups. "He's almost out!"

Hector sped up, holding the snowball with his antennae and using all six feet to push. Suddenly the ice behind him sank with a sickening lurch.

"Uncle Hector, watch out!"

Hector spun around just in time to see the ant lion, dripping with snow, raise his pincers overhead. He pushed Lulu's snowball toward the shore with all his might and leaped after it, but the ant lion grabbed his leg and pulled him back.

"*Uuuh!*" Hector grunted, falling flat on his belly.

"Hold on! Hold on!" yelled the wumblepups. They scrambled out onto the ice and grabbed Hector's front legs. Down, down! The ant lion pulled Hector toward the middle of the stream. Up, up! The pups yanked as hard as they could, but the ant lion was stronger than all of them. Suddenly there came a great tug from above, and Hector felt he would be torn in two.

"Harder, pups! Pull!" It was Cosmo, joining the pups.

Crack! Hector's leg snapped. He flew toward the stream bank.

The ant lion fell back. *Splash!* The ice broke and he pitched backward into the shadows, into the freezing water—pincers, barbs, jaws, and all.

Chapter Fourteen

Wumblebug Theater

"**F**amily and friends!" cried Cosmo. "The show is about to begin!"

In the new wumblebug hole, the winter party was in full swing. All sorts of small creatures—ladybugs and fireflies, crickets and snails, centipedes and roly-polies, and stinkbugs and spiders—crowded through the new entry tunnel where the ant lion had once slept. They gathered in the great hall, hung with pine tips and red berries and scales from the wings of butterflies, glittering in the firelight.

Hector sat in his big chair, resting his sore leg on the piano bench. At his side sat Suzy and Lance. In front of them all, Cosmo hopped down from a stage as a wumblepup peeked

66

out from a leaf curtain, then vanished again.

The candles went out and all eyes focused on the stage.

A large, dark figure in cape and hood appeared from the shadows. Suddenly the hood flew back. Six eyes gleamed from a bushy beard. Some of the smaller guests gasped as the spider—a wolf spider—stepped to the center and began to speak in a deep, growling voice.

Bugs and spiders, large and small,
Welcome to this spacious hall.
Tonight we bring you tales of daring!
Tales of travel, tales worth sharing!
Tales of Hector Fuller, so . . .
Take your seats and enjoy the show!

The wolf spider swirled his cape and disappeared. The curtain jerked aside, revealing a stage set of Hector's hole with wumblepups jumping and bouncing everywhere.

Lulu stood in the center. On her back was Hector's old pack, and on her shoulders was his scarf. "It's too noisy in here!" she said. "I'm leaving."

She marched in a circle and then lay down. The pups ran off. When they came back, each held pieces of dandelion fluff. They fluttered over Lulu, waving the fluff like snowflakes falling from the sky. Then they dragged her away as the curtain fell.

Hector chuckled and clapped. "I was looking for that scarf," he whispered to Suzy.

"Look," said Suzy. "They're starting again."

The curtain opened on a dark stage wrapped with a big, brown leaf to look like the walls of a tunnel. Into one end of the tunnel came Lulu. Into the other came Gin.

"Gin!" said Lulu. "Where have you been?"

Gin stared at the audience. "Umm . . . I . . . uh . . ."

"Shortcuts are dangerous," said Lulu in a

serious voice. "You should—"

"*Yaaargh!*" Bursting through the tunnel came a tall, strange shape—Otis's legs at the bottom and Oscar's above and Globug at the top, all wrapped in bark with twigs sticking out like the pincers of the ant lion. The creature chased Lulu and Gin into the crowd of guests, who screamed and laughed and fell off their chairs.

"Now this is what I call a party," said Cosmo, catching Lulu for a hug as she dashed by.

"The greatest party ever!" yelled Lulu. "Here, Uncle Hector." She started to squirm out of Hector's backpack.

"Keep it," said Hector. "You keep it, until the next trip."

Lulu ran to join the other pups, dancing on the stage.

With a sweep of his cape, the wolf spider gathered them into a bow. Then his deep voice filled the room again.

Here they are, ladies and gents.
Wumblebug Theater presents
Our stars—the wumblepups and their
mother!
Directed by myself, no other!
Performing for you who gather here . . .
And don't forget to come back next year . . .
Now let us raise a cup of nectar
To our host—and cheers to Hector!

The crowd stood on their feet and cheered.

"You're a good bug, Hector," whispered Suzy.

Hector Fuller spread his short wing over his cousin's spotted shoulder, and together they watched the wumblepups dance in the light of the fire.

Ready-for-Chapters

Enjoy the very best first chapter book fiction in Ready-for-Chapters books from Aladdin Paperbacks.

Aladdin Paperbacks

Simon & Schuster Children's Publishing • www.SimonSaysKids.com